T0144035

MY MOM, MY HERO

WRITTEN BY VALERIE CAMACHO

To order additional copies of this book, contact:
Xlibris
844-714-8691
www.Xlibris.com
Orders@Xlibris.com

ISBN:	Softcover	978-1-6641-7004-9
	EBook	978-1-6641-7005-6

Print information available on the last page

Rev. date: 04/15/2021

RISE AND SHINE, ITS

vIL DOG TiME!!!

TIME TO GET UP AND BRUSH YOUR TEETH.
BRUSH YOUR HAIR.
AND MAKE SURE YOU ARE WEARING CLEAN UNDERWEAR.

TIME TO GO, MOMMA HAS TO WORK, MARINES ARE WAITING ON HER TO TEACH THEM TEAMWORK.

TIME TO RUN, MOMMA SINGS CADENCE WITH HER MARINES FOR FUN.

LOOK TO THE RIGHT AND WHAT DO I SEE, A SCHOOL FULL OF KIDS STARING AT ME.

SCHOOL IS OUT! KIDS RUN HOME LIKE THEY ARE GOING TO EXPLODE, WHILE MOMMA S GUARD THE ROAD.

FRIENDS ARE OUR FAMILY,
SINCE WE ARE SO FAR AWAY.
MOMMA IS A MARINE,
AND SHE WILL MAKE YOUR DAY.

ppy Birthday!!!
IT S TIME TO CELEBRATE YOUR BIRTHDAY WITH ALL YOUR FRIENDS FROM CLASS.
FIRST THING IS A GAME IN THE GRASS.

GAME AFTER GAME,
XBOY
YEET!
XBOY
XBOY

OUR FRIENDS WIN PRIZES OF ALL DIFFERENT SIZES.

HAPPY HAPPY BiRTHDAY! HAPPY HAPPY BiRTHDAY! HAPPY BiRTHDAY TO YOU!

CAKE AND ICE CREAM TIME, WE WANT TO BUST THE PINATA, THE BEST PART OF TURNING NINE.

CANDY AND PRIZES FLY THREW THE AIR!
AS THE BIRTHDAY BOY BREAKS THE GIANT BEAR.

THE PARTY CAME TO AN END, MOMMA CLEANED UP THE HOUSE WHILE YOU PLAYED WITH YOUR BEST FRIEND.

FIRST GRANDMA AND GRANDPA, THEN AUNTIE AND UNCLE,
BUT YOUR MOST FAVORITE OF THEM ALL WERE YOUR COUSINS HAPPY BIRTHDAY CALL.

IT IS TIME FOR BED, TOMORROW IS A NEW ADVENTURE.
WE ARE IN HAWAII, WE WILL GO EXPLORE NATURE.
The Proud
The Few
The Brave

The Proud
The Few
The Brave
MARINES
UNTIL TOMORROW, I LOVE YOU KIDDO.
GOOD NIGHT MOMMA, YOU ARE MY SUPERHERO!
Math
Oscar the Tiger Shark

Printed in the United States
by Baker & Taylor Publisher Services